Remarkable Writers

A. A. Milne

Anita Yasuda

MEDIA ENHANCED BOOKS
AV2 BY WEIGL™
ADDED VALUE • AUDIO VISUAL

www.av2books.com

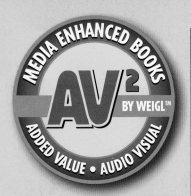

AV² provides enriched content that supplements and complements this book. Weigl's AV² books strive to create inspired learning and engage young minds in a total learning experience.

Your AV² Media Enhanced books come alive with...

Audio
Listen to sections of the book read aloud.

Key Words
Study vocabulary, and complete a matching word activity.

Video
Watch informative video clips.

Quizzes
Test your knowledge.

Embedded Weblinks
Gain additional information for research.

Slide Show
View images and captions, and prepare a presentation.

Try This!
Complete activities and hands-on experiments.

... and much, much more!

Go to **www.av2books.com**, and enter this book's unique code.

BOOK CODE

V908780

AV² by Weigl brings you media enhanced books that support active learning.

Published by AV² by Weigl
350 5th Avenue, 59th Floor
New York, NY 10118

Website: www.weigl.com www.av2books.com
Copyright ©2014 AV² by Weigl

Library of Congress Cataloging-in-Publication Data

Yasuda, Anita.
  A. A. Milne / Anita Yasuda.
    pages cm. -- (Remarkable Writers)
  Includes index.
  ISBN 978-1-62127-401-8 (hardcover : alk. paper) -- ISBN 978-1-62127-407-0 (softcover : alk. paper)
  1. Milne, A. A. (Alan Alexander), 1882-1956. 2. Authors, English--20th century--Biography--Juvenile literature. 3. Children's stories--Authorship--Juvenile literature. I. Title.
  PR6025.I65Z99 2014
  828'.91209--dc23
   [B]
                          2012040841

Printed in the United States of America, in North Mankato, Minnesota
1 2 3 4 5 6 7 8 9 0 17 16 15 14 13

012013
WEP301112

Senior Editor: Heather Kissock
Design: Terry Paulhus

Weigl acknowledges Getty Images as its primary photo supplier for this title.

Contents

Introducing A. A. Milne

A. A. Milne was a British poet, **playwright**, and author whose work was popular all over the world. From the early 1900s to the late 1950s, Milne wrote more than 30 plays, along with several poems and novels. However, he is best remembered for his works for children. These stories introduced the world to Christopher Robin and his teddy bear, Winnie-the-Pooh.

Milne used both **prose** and poetry when writing his books. His words make readers smile at the innocent views his characters have of their world. Many people recognize his characters' **catch phrases**, such as "Silly old bear!," and "Oh, bother!," even if they have never read Milne's books.

More than 75 years after being created, Milne's Winnie-the-Pooh characters continue to entertain children of all ages through books, movies, and television shows.

Milne's **inspiration** for his children's books came from many sources. He drew upon his own childhood memories of growing up in London as well as the experiences of his son, Christopher Robin, and his much-loved teddy bear. Milne said that he did not create the world of Winnie-the-Pooh. He only described it.

Milne developed the Winnie-the-Pooh books by watching Christopher Robin play with his teddy bear.

Today, Milne's children's books are still read and loved by people in many countries. Their enduring theme of the importance of friendship continues to attract new readers all over the world. The books are so popular that, in 2011, Winnie-the-Pooh celebrated his 90th anniversary. Events marking this beloved character and his creator, A. A. Milne, were held around the globe.

Writing A Biography

Writers are often inspired to record the stories of people who lead interesting lives. The story of another person's life is called a biography. A biography can tell the story of any person, from authors such as A. A. Milne, to inventors, presidents, and sports stars.

When writing a biography, authors must first collect information about their subject. This information may come from a book about the person's life, a news article about one of his or her accomplishments, or a review of his or her work. Libraries and the internet will have much of this information. Most biographers will also interview their subjects. Personal accounts provide a great deal of information and a unique point of view. When some basic details about the person's life have been collected, it is time to begin writing a biography.

As you read about A. A. Milne, you will be introduced to the important parts of a biography. Use these tips and the examples provided to learn how to write about an author or any other remarkable person.

Early Life

Alan Alexander Milne was born on January 18, 1882, in England. He grew up in Kilburn, a community in the north part of London. His father, John, was a schoolteacher. His mother, Sarah, had run a school for young ladies prior to her marriage. Alan was the youngest of three children. He had two older brothers, David and Kenneth.

"Father and Mother had always determined that there should be no favourites in their family. The three of us were to be treated alike…"
— A.A. Milne

John and Sarah encouraged their sons to learn. The Milne home was full of books, pictures, and even an aquarium. Every night, John would read to his sons before putting them to bed. Alan and his brothers gathered in the nursery each evening, eagerly waiting for their father to read a chapter of a book to them.

Before Alan and his brothers went to kindergarten, their father had large **sight-reading** sheets put up around the nursery. Their **governess** used them to teach the boys how to read. Alan was a fast learner and was able to read by the age of three.

Kilburn is known for its large Irish population. Many of the people living there are either from Ireland or have Irish roots.

When they were older, the boys attended their father's private boys' school. Named Henley House, the school had about 50 pupils. One of the teachers at Henley House was H. G. Wells, who taught Alan science. Wells would later become a well-known science-fiction writer.

Alan showed an interest in words from an early age. He enjoyed writing about what was going on around him. When he was only eight years old, the Henley House school magazine published Alan's first article. It described a competition between boys at the school.

Alan studied hard to get good grades. His efforts were rewarded when, at age 11, he was given a **scholarship** to study at Westminster School. Westminster is one of England's most respected high schools. Many of its students go on to study at top universities.

🖉 H. G. Wells was an important mentor to Alan. He encouraged Alan's writing and helped him with his career.

Growing Up

Alan appreciated the opportunity to study at Westminster. He remained focused on getting good grades and worked toward that goal. Alan could often be found in the school library during the evenings, studying for class. He excelled at mathematics and belonged to the school's Literary Society and its Debating Society.

It was only when he was nearing the end of his schooling at Westminster that Alan realized he loved writing. While at his parents' home for Christmas, a visitor started to write a poem for Alan's brother, Ken. Alan helped her to finish the poem, and they sent it to his brother. When Ken wrote back in **verse**, he challenged Alan to do the same. For the next two years, Alan and Ken wrote verse together.

During this time, the brothers also began writing for their school magazine, *The Elizabethan*. They wrote poetry and **parodies** under the initials A. K. M. These initials came from a combination of their names.

Get to Know England

North Sea

SCOTLAND

IRELAND

ENGLAND

WALES

London

Atlantic Ocean

English Channel

LEGEND

England
Borders
Land
Capital City
Water

SCALE 0
50 Km   50 Miles

Alan had great fun contributing to *The Elizabethan*, but he thought of writing as a hobby. He did not think that it would one day be his job. He planned to go to Oxford or Cambridge University and study mathematics.

Then, something happened that changed Alan's course. A copy of the Cambridge student magazine *The Granta* arrived at Westminster. One of his friends suggested that Alan should try to become an **editor** for the magazine. That was when Alan decided to attend Cambridge University.

Writing About
Growing Up

Some people know what they want to achieve in life from a very young age. Others do not decide until much later. In any case, it is important for biographers to discuss when and how their subjects make these decisions. Using the information they collect, biographers try to answer the following questions about their subjects' paths in life.

1 Who had the most influence on the person?

2 Did he or she receive assistance from others?

3 Did the person have a positive attitude?

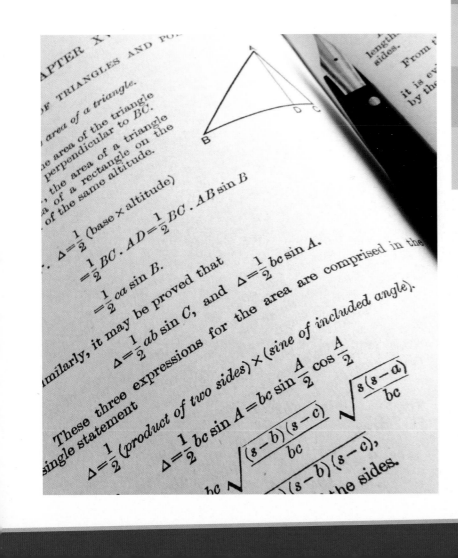

Mathematics is a core subject at school. Core subjects are considered to be the bases for all other learning. The other core subjects are language arts, science, and social studies.

Developing Skills

In 1900, Alan received a scholarship to study mathematics at Cambridge University. He began making plans to attend the prestigious school. However, he told his friends that he was really going to Cambridge to become the editor of *The Granta*.

"My friend... and I stood looking at this copy of *The Granta*, and suddenly he said, 'You ought to go to Cambridge and edit that.' So I said quite firmly, 'I will.'" —*A. A. Milne*

Once at Cambridge, Alan and his brother Ken continued to work together on their writing. They set to work **submitting** verses and other writings to the magazine. At first, nothing was accepted.

Alan and Ken did not give up. They sent in their work every week and waited patiently to hear from the magazine's publisher. Finally, during Alan's second term, *The Granta* accepted one of their poems.

Cambridge University is the seventh oldest university in the world.

The brothers continued contributing verses, but over time, the partnership came to an end. Alan began submitting work to the magazine under his own name, A. A. Milne. At first, he was afraid that his work might be rejected. Instead, he was asked to become *The Granta's* new editor. Alan agreed without hesitation. He remained editor of the magazine until his graduation in 1903.

During Alan's last year at Cambridge, he devoted much of his time to studying for his math exams, but he did not do as well as expected. Alan's father was not pleased with his results. Still, he hoped that Alan would pursue a career in teaching or the **civil service**. This was not to happen. By this time, Alan knew what he wanted to do with his life.

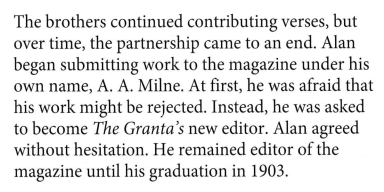

📖 As the editor of *The Granta*, Alan had to write a weekly editorial about topics related to the university.

Every remarkable person has skills and traits that make him or her noteworthy. Some people have natural talent, while others practice diligently. For most, it is a combination of the two. One of the most important things that a biographer can do is to tell the story of how the subject developed his or her talents.

1 What was the person's education?

2 What was the person's first job or work experience?

3 What obstacles did the person overcome?

Timeline of A. A. Milne

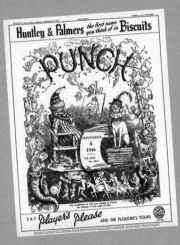

1906
Alan becomes an assistant editor at *Punch* magazine.

1882
Alan Alexander Milne is born in England on January 18, 1882 to John and Sarah Milne.

1903
Alan moves to London to become a writer. His work is published in *Vanity Fair*.

1900
Alan attends Trinity College, which is part of Cambridge University. Here, he becomes editor-in-chief of its humor magazine, *The Granta*. After three years, Alan graduates with a degree in mathematics.

1913

Alan marries Dorothy "Daphne" de Sélincourt, the goddaughter of the editor of *Punch*.

2011

A new movie about Winnie-the-Pooh is released. *Winnie-the-Pooh* wins an Annie Award, animation's highest honor.

1923

Alan writes a children's poem entitled "Vespers," using his infant son as inspiration.

1966

Winnie the Pooh and the Honey Tree, the first short film based on Alan's characters, is released by The Walt Disney Company.

Early Achievements

After Alan did poorly on his final exams at Cambridge, he told his father that he wanted to be a writer. His father was concerned about this career choice. He knew that writers did not make much money.

Alan remained committed to becoming a **professional** writer. He moved to London, where many of the country's **publishing** companies were. There, he spent most of his time writing. As soon as he completed a piece of writing, he would send it to newspapers and magazines, and wait for a response.

His writing soon attracted attention. Before the year ended, *Vanity Fair* magazine bought an article Alan had written about detective Sherlock Holmes. The magazine paid Alan 15 shillings, or $1.50 U.S., for his work.

As rewarding as this was, Alan's dream was to be published in a British humor magazine called *Punch*. Every week, he submitted writings to *Punch*, and each time they were rejected. In 1904, the magazine finally agreed to publish a set of verses Alan had written.

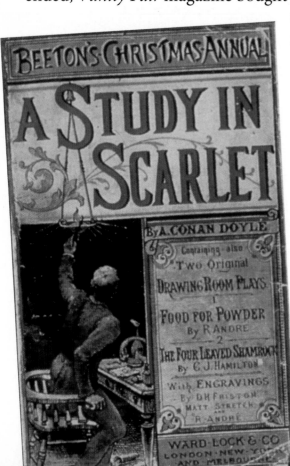

✍ The detective Sherlock Homes is a famous fictional character developed by the author Sir Arthur Conan Doyle. The character was first introduced in *A Study in Scarlet* in 1887.

Alan's writing was soon appearing in other magazines and newspapers. *The Daily News* and *The Westminster Gazette* published his essays and stories. The editors at *The Evening News* asked him to write for them on a weekly basis. Shortly after, Alan received an offer from *The Daily Mail* to work as an editor at the newspaper.

Then, Alan received an offer he could not refuse. The editors at *Punch* asked him to work for them as an assistant editor. Alan had long been a fan of the magazine, so working there was a dream come true. While working for *Punch*, Alan published his first book, *The Day's Play*. It was a collection of articles he had written for the magazine.

While working at *Punch*, Alan met Dorothy "Daphne" de Sélincourt. She was the goddaughter of the magazine's editor, Owen Seaman, and a big fan of Alan's work. In 1913, Alan and Daphne were married.

The following year, World War I began. Alan joined the army and was sent to France. After leaving the army, Alan decided that he did not want to return to his job at *Punch*. Instead, he wanted to write plays.

Writing About
Early Achievements

No two people take the same path to success. Some people work very hard for a long time before achieving their goals. Others may take advantage of a fortunate turn of events. Biographers must make special note of the traits and qualities that allow their subjects to succeed.

1 What was the person's most important early success?

2 What processes does the person use in his or her work?

3 Which of the person's traits was most helpful in his or her work?

Milne joined the army as a signaling officer. This means he worked with telegraph equipment and other communications systems.

Tricks of the Trade

Writing a story or a poem can be challenging, but it can also be very rewarding. Some writers have trouble coming up with ideas, while others have so many ideas that they do not know where to begin. A. A. Milne had special writing habits that young writers can follow in order to develop their own ideas and stories.

Keep Your Eyes and Ears Open

Many writers get ideas by watching people and listening to conversations. If you pay attention, you will see that most people say and do all sorts of interesting things. These things can inspire writers to develop characters or to write funny scenes. Alan found inspiration in the people and things close to him, including his son Christopher Robin and his stuffed animals. Alan would use his imagination to create amusing adventures for them.

Christopher Robin's stuffed animal collection can be seen at the New York Public Library. The display allows people to see the toys that inspired Milne to write the Winnie-the-Pooh stories.

Write, Write, Write

Sometimes, the easiest way to finish a poem or a story is to write as much as possible in a first **draft**. This way, a writer can get all his or her ideas down on paper. The writer can then review what has been written and decide which parts to keep. Very few writers have produced a great story in just one draft. Most go over their text and make changes until they are satisfied with the way it reads. Alan always made sure that he wrote at least 1,000 words each day.

"...there is no artistic reward for a book written for children other than the knowledge that they enjoy it." —A. A. Milne

The Creative Process

Each writer has his or her own approach to the writing process. Some writers need to make a detailed outline. This is a good idea for new writers, as it will help them to organize their thoughts. Some writers do not use an outline. They simply begin writing and let their ideas flow. Alan had no set pattern to his creative process. Sometimes, he would write a few lines of verse at a time, and not have an entire book completed for a year. When writing his plays, Alan enjoyed writing all the **dialogue** at once.

It Takes Dedication

Writing takes dedication and discipline. Alan spent hours working on his poems and stories, only taking brief breaks for meals. He continued to write even when his work was rejected. It was this dedication that allowed Alan to create a variety of books in so many **genres**.

Several of Milne's plays had successful runs in London theaters. In 1937, Milne's comedy called *Sarah Simple* was performed at the Garrick Theatre in London.

Remarkable Books

Alan had a long writing career as a poet, playwright, and children's author. Although most of his plays and essays were written for adults, people of all ages are familiar with Milne's works for young readers. Many parents are reminded of their own childhood when they read A. A. Milne's books with their children.

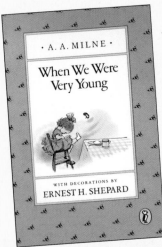

When We Were Very Young

When We Were Very Young is a collection of poetry and verses for children. It begins by explaining that the poems feature characters who are friends of Milne's son, Christopher Robin. One of the poems in the book is entitled "Teddy Bear." It is one of the first appearances of Winnie-the-Pooh in print. The poem describes the bear as growing tubby no matter how hard he tries. Ernest H. Shepard illustrated *When We Were Very Young*. He worked with Milne at *Punch* magazine and later illustrated many more of Milne's children's books.

A Gallery of Children

A Gallery of Children contains 12 short-stories told in verse and prose. Some of the stories include "The Princess and the Apple Tree," "A Voyage to India," and "Castles by the Sea." Each story retells a child's adventure and is accompanied by beautiful illustrations by Dutch artist Henriette Willebeek le Mair. Colgate had originally **commissioned** the illustrations in 1925 for magazine advertising. A. A. Milne was inspired by the illustrations and used them as the basis of these short stories.

Winnie-the-Pooh

Winnie-the-Pooh is a book about a cute bear called Pooh who lives in the Hundred Acre Wood. Pooh has two loves in life—honey and his friends. The book begins with a description of Christopher Robin dragging poor Winnie-the-Pooh down the staircase with a bump-bump-bump. Winnie-the-Pooh then sets out on a quest for honey in a tree that is said to be "buzzing and buzzing" with bees. Winnie-the-Pooh tells the reader that honey is only made so that he can eat it. After a disastrous climb up the tree, Winnie-the-Pooh lands with a thump at Christopher Robin's feet. The rest of the book includes tales of Winnie-the-Pooh and Piglet hunting Woozles, Eeyore the donkey losing his tail, and Piglet meeting a Heffalump.

AWARDS
Winnie-the-Pooh
2000 Millennium Book Award
2012 *Junior* Magazine's Best Classic Book Award

· A. A. MILNE ·

Winnie-the-Pooh

WITH DECORATIONS BY
ERNEST H. SHEPARD

Now We Are Six

Now We are Six is a collection of 35 children's poems. In the book's playful introduction, Alan explains that it has taken him nearly three years to write the book. He tells the reader that Pooh only stumbled upon the book by accident when he was looking for his friend Piglet. Some of the best-known poems from this book include "Solitude," in which a young boy describes the joys of being all alone in a playhouse, "King John's Christmas," a poem about a man who wanted Father Christmas to bring him a gift, and "Furry Bear," in which the author describes the joys of being a bear who sleeps through the winter.

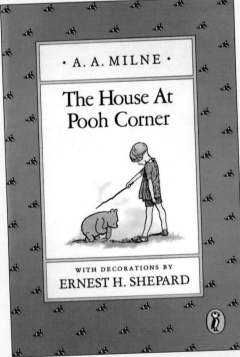

The House at Pooh Corner

This book is about the importance of friendship. In this second collection of Pooh stories, the reader finds Winnie-the-Pooh waiting for Piglet on a snowy day. Winnie-the-Pooh is trying to stay warm by jumping up and down and humming his 'Tiddely Pom' song. At Pooh's suggestion, the two friends decide to build Eeyore the donkey a home at Pooh Corner. Pooh and Piglet are delighted to find a large pile of sticks that they can use. They are later surprised to find out that the pile of sticks was in fact already Eeyore's home.

Toad of Toad Hall

In 1929, Alan adapted Kenneth Grahame's book *The Wind in the Willows* into a play called *Toad of Toad Hall.* By a quiet riverbank, the lives of Mole, Rat, and Badger are interrupted by Toad's fun-loving pranks. One day, Toad decides to go for a walk in the country. During his jaunt, he finds a car that is too beautiful to resist. He decides to take it for a ride, even though the car does not belong to him. When the police find Toad, he is sent to jail for stealing the car. Toad is not there for long, however, as he finds a way to escape. When he returns home, he is shocked to find Toad Hall occupied by his enemies from the Wild Wood, including a ferret and a weasel. Toad's friends, Mole, Rat, and Badger, help him to win back his house.

The play debuted at the Lyric Theater in London on December 17, 1929 and was well received by audiences and critics. *Toad of Toad Hall* remains popular, and the play is still often staged today.

From Big Ideas to Books

In 1920, Alan and Dorothy welcomed the birth of their only son Christopher Robin. A few years later, Alan wrote a poem about Christopher Robin entitled "Vespers." He gave it to Dorothy as a gift. Dorothy loved the poem and wanted to share it with others. She sent it to magazines to see if they would publish it. It was eventually published in *Vanity Fair*. Before long, Alan was being asked to write more poems for children.

"It has been my good fortune as a writer that what I have wanted to write has for the most part proved to be saleable."
—A. A. Milne

When Christopher Robin was three years old, the family rented a home in Wales. As he watched his son playing, Alan began to think about his own childhood. His memories inspired him to write more children's verses. These poems were published in a book called *When We Were Very Young*. It became a bestseller both in England and the United States.

One of the most touching verses in the book is called "Teddy Bear." For many readers, "Teddy Bear" was their introduction to Winnie-the-Pooh. Alan soon began to write more stories about the little bear.

The Publishing Process

Publishing companies receive hundreds of **manuscripts** from authors each year. Only a few manuscripts become books. Publishers must be sure that a manuscript will sell many copies. As a result, publishers reject most of the manuscripts they receive. Once a manuscript has been accepted, it goes through

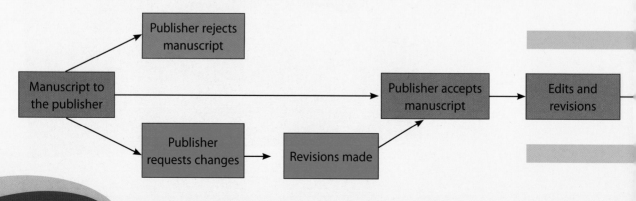

In 1925, the bear appeared in a story called "The Wrong Sort of Bees," published in the *London Evening News*. People loved the story so much that Alan was asked to write a book featuring Winnie-the-Pooh. "The Wrong Sort of Bees" became the first chapter of *Winnie-the-Pooh*, a collection of stories about Pooh and his friends. In its first year, the book sold 150,000 copies in the United States alone.

Milne's good friend, artist Ernest H. Shepard, illustrated the original Winnie-the-Pooh books with wonderful drawings that brought Pooh and his friends to life.

Alan's inspiration for the stories came from Christopher Robin and his collection of stuffed animals. The teddy bear was named after a real bear that Christopher Robin liked to visit at the London Zoo. Winnie the black bear was so tame that Christopher was even allowed to go into its cage. Other stuffed animals in Christopher's collection inspired the rest of the characters in *Winnie-the-Pooh*. These included a donkey named Eeyore and a stuffed pig called Piglet.

many stages before it is published. Often, authors change their work to follow an editor's suggestions. Once the book is published, some authors receive royalties. This is money based on book sales.

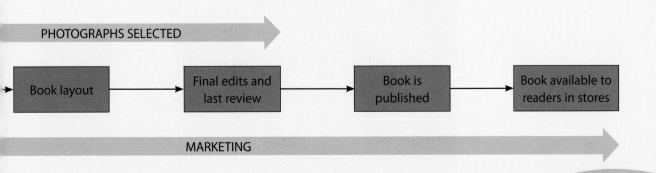

PHOTOGRAPHS SELECTED

Book layout → Final edits and last review → Book is published → Book available to readers in stores

MARKETING

A. A. Milne Today

In 1925, Alan and Dorothy Milne bought Cotchford Farm, in Hartfield, East Sussex, England. The local countryside served as the inspiration for the Winnie-the-Pooh books. After suffering a **stroke** in 1952, Alan retired from writing and spent his days living quietly on his farm. He died on January 31, 1956.

Five years later, The Walt Disney Company purchased the right to develop new projects using the Winnie-the-Pooh characters. Since 1961, the little bear and his friends have been featured in many animated movies, television shows, and stage productions. Disney has also developed many products that feature Winnie-the-Pooh characters. This **merchandise** has earned The Walt Disney Company more than $1 billion. Disney pays royalties to the **Royal Literary Fund** for the use of the Pooh characters. The Fund's Fellowship Scheme uses this money to help British authors who are having financial difficulties. The program also helps to place professional writers in British colleges and universities.

On April 11, 2006, Winnie-the-Pooh received a star on the Hollywood Walk of Fame. The award paid tribute to the character's long history in the entertainment industry.

As a tribute to Alan, the people of Sussex often refer to Cotchford Farm as Pooh Corner. The farm features a statue of Christopher Robin in the garden, a sundial engraved with the initials A. A. M., and carvings of several Pooh characters. Many places in the Pooh books are based on locations in the area. It is common for fans to stop on Pooh Bridge and play a game of poohsticks, just like Winnie-the-Pooh did in *The House at Pooh Corner*. To play, competitors drop wooden sticks off the bridge and then wait to see whose stick will cross the finish line first.

Today, *Winnie-the-Pooh* remains a classic in children's **literature**. Parents and children alike still feel a connection to the book's whimsical characters. *Winnie-the-Pooh* has been translated into more than 50 languages, including Yiddish, Japanese, Latin, and Mongolian.

In 1999, Pooh Bridge was showing signs of wear and had to be completely rebuilt. Today, the bridge continues to be a popular spot for a game of poohsticks.

Writing About the Person Today

The biography of any living person is an ongoing story. People have new ideas, start new projects, and deal with challenges. For their work to be meaningful, biographers must include up-to-date information about their subjects. Through research, biographers try to answer the following questions.

1 Has the person received awards or recognition for accomplishments?

2 What is the person's life's work?

3 How have the person's accomplishments served others?

Fan Information

Alan wrote children's books that made readers want to be a part of the story. Millions of fans love the adorable bear Winnie-the-Pooh, Eeyore the grumpy donkey, and the bouncing Tigger. Alan received many letters from fans who wanted to tell him how much they loved his stories. He was disappointed that he could not respond to all the letters.

Once Christopher Robin grew up, Alan stopped writing children's books. Instead, he began to focus on writing plays. The characters from the Pooh books continue to live on, however. Fans have created new ways to honor Winnie-the-Pooh and his friends.

✍ Fans can visit the characters from Winnie-the-Pooh at several Walt Disney amusement parks. Some of the parks also have a ride based on the Winnie-the-Pooh stories.

On January 18, people around the world celebrate Winnie-the-Pooh Day. This date was chosen because it is the birthdate of both Alan and his little bear. Fans devote the day to Pooh-inspired events. They read Winnie-the-Pooh books, make crafts, sing songs from the books and movies, and host parties in which Pooh's favorite snacks, tea and honey, are served.

In England, the annual World Poohsticks Championships are held on the Thames River, near the town of Dorchester-on-Thames, in Oxfordshire. Competitors can take part in either individual or team events. All competitors must follow "The official Pooh Corner Rules for Playing Poohsticks." These rules were written in 1996 to commemorate the 70th anniversary of *Winnie-the-Pooh*.

A. A. Milne fans have created impressive websites to share information. To find websites on A. A. Milne and his work, type "A. A. Milne" or "Winnie-the-Pooh" into search engines on the internet.

In 2009, a new Winnie-the-Pooh book was published. Written by David Benedictus, *Return to the Hundred Acre Wood* includes all of the original characters and introduces a new character, Lottie the Otter, to Winnie-the-Pooh fans.

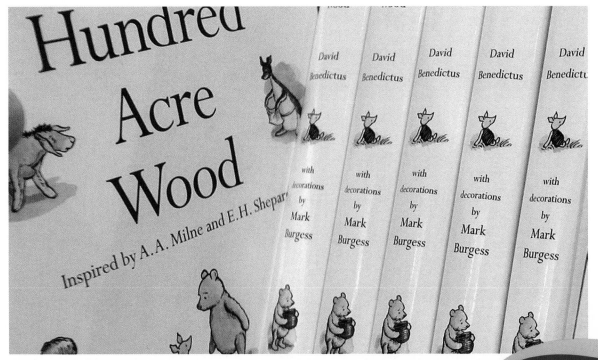

Write a Biography

All of the parts of a biography work together to tell the story of a person's life. Find out how these elements combine by writing a biography. Begin by choosing a person whose story fascinates you. You will have to research the person's life by using library books and reliable websites. You can also e-mail the person or write him or her a letter. The person might agree to answer your questions directly.

Use a concept web, such as the one below, to guide you in writing the biography. Answer each of the questions listed using the information you have gathered. Each heading on the concept web will form an important part of the person's story.

Parts of a Biography

Early Life

Where and when was the person born?

What is known about the person's family and friends?

Did the person grow up in unusual circumstances?

Growing Up

Who had the most influence on the person?

Did he or she receive assistance from others?

Did the person have a positive attitude?

Developing Skills

What was the person's education?

What was the person's first job or work experience?

What obstacles did the person overcome?

Person Today

Has the person received awards or recognition for accomplishments?

What is the person's life's work?

How have the person's accomplishments served others?

Early Achievements

What was the person's most important early success?

What processes does the person use in his or her work?

Which of the person's traits were most helpful in his or her work?

Test Yourself

1 Where and when was A. A. Milne born?

2 By what age had Alan learned to read?

3 What did Alan and his brother Ken enjoy writing together?

4 What was the name of Alan's first school?

5 What magazine did Alan edit while at university?

6 What subject did Alan excel in at school?

7 What was the name of the magazine Alan worked for when he graduated from Cambridge?

8 Why did Alan name his main character Winnie?

9 What is the name of the company that bought the rights to Winnie-the-Pooh?

10 When is Winnie-the-Pooh Day?

ANSWERS
1. A. A. Milne was born in England on January 18, 1882. 2. Alan knew how to read by the time he was three years old. 3. Alan and Ken liked to write verse together. 4. Alan's first school was called Henley House. 5. Alan was the editor of *The Granta*. 6. Mathematics was Alan's strongest subject in school. 7. Alan wrote for *Punch* after leaving university. 8. His son had a teddy bear called Winnie that was named after a bear at the London Zoo. 9. The Walt Disney Company bought the rights to Winnie-the-Pooh. 10. Winnie-the-Pooh Day is celebrated on January 18.

Writing Terms

The field of writing has its own language. Understanding some of the more common writing terms will allow you to discuss your ideas about books.

action: the moving events of a work of fiction

antagonist: the person in the story who opposes the main character

autobiography: a history of a person's life written by that person

biography: a written account of another person's life

character: a person in a story, poem, or play

climax: the most exciting moment or turning point in a story

episode: a scene or short piece of action in a story

fiction: stories about characters and events that are not real

foreshadow: hinting at something that is going to happen later in the book

imagery: a written description of a thing or idea that brings an image to mind

narrator: the speaker of the story who relates the events

nonfiction: writing that deals with real people and events

novel: published writing of considerable length that portrays characters within a story

plot: the order of events in a work of fiction

protagonist: the leading character of a story; often a likable character

resolution: the end of the story, when the conflict is settled

scene: a single episode in a story

setting: the place and time in which a work of fiction occurs

theme: an idea that runs throughout a work of fiction

Key Words

catch phrases: two or more words which are repeated often

civil service: body of government employees entrusted with the administration of the country

commissioned: authorized the production of something

dialogue: conversation between characters in a book or movie

draft: a rough copy of a story

editor: a person who is in charge of and determines the final content of a text

genres: categories into which pieces of writing fit

governess: a woman employed to teach the children of a private household

inspiration: something or someone that generates an idea in another person

literature: writing of lasting value, including plays, poems, and novels

manuscripts: drafts of stories before they are published

merchandise: goods which are sold

parodies: humorous imitations of serious works of literature

playwright: a person who writes plays

professional: following an occupation as a means of making a living

prose: ordinary speech or writing

publishing: the business of issuing printed matter for sale

Royal Literary Fund: an organization that helps published authors who are struggling financially

scholarship: financial aid awarded to a student

sight-reading: words which can be recognized right away

stroke: a sudden loss of brain function caused by a blockage or rupture of a blood vessel to the brain

submitting: handing something in

verse: writing arranged with a rhythm and usually a rhyme

Index

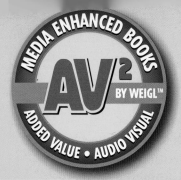

Log on to www.av2books.com

AV² by Weigl brings you media enhanced books that support active learning. Go to www.av2books.com, and enter the special code found on page 2 of this book. You will gain access to enriched and enhanced content that supplements and complements this book. Content includes video, audio, weblinks, quizzes, a slide show, and activities.

AV² Online Navigation

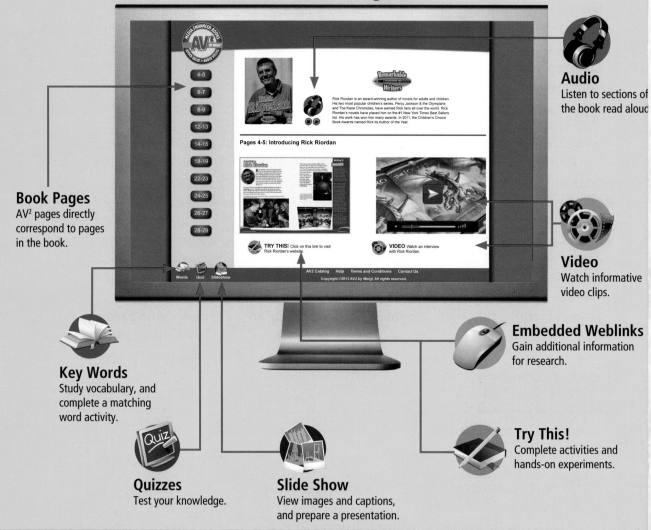

Book Pages
AV² pages directly correspond to pages in the book.

Audio
Listen to sections of the book read aloud.

Video
Watch informative video clips.

Embedded Weblinks
Gain additional information for research.

Try This!
Complete activities and hands-on experiments.

Key Words
Study vocabulary, and complete a matching word activity.

Quizzes
Test your knowledge.

Slide Show
View images and captions, and prepare a presentation.

AV² was built to bridge the gap between print and digital. We encourage you to tell us what you like and what you want to see in the future.

Sign up to be an AV² Ambassador at www.av2books.com/ambassador.